Mary Rayner

The Echoing Green

Illustrated by Michael Foreman

PUFFIN BOOKS

PUFFIN BOOKS

Published by the Penguin Group
Penguin Books Ltd, 27 Wrights Lane, London W8 5TZ, England
Penguin Books USA Inc., 375 Hudson Street, New York, New York 10014, USA
Penguin Books Australia Ltd, Ringwood, Victoria, Australia
Penguin Books Canada Ltd, 10 Alcorn Avenue, Toronto, Ontario, Canada M4V 3B2
Penguin Books (NZ) Ltd, 182–190 Wairau Road, Auckland 10, New Zealand

Penguin Books Ltd, Registered Offices: Harmondsworth, Middlesex, England

First published by Viking 1992
Published in Puffin Books 1994
1 3 5 7 9 10 8 6 4 2

Text copyright © Mary Rayner, 1992
Illustrations copyright © Michael Foreman, 1992
All rights reserved

The moral right of the author and illustrator has been asserted

Printed in England by Clays Ltd, St Ives plc
Filmset in Palatino

Except in the United States of America, this book is sold subject
to the condition that it shall not, by way of trade or otherwise, be lent,
re-sold, hired out, or otherwise circulated without the publisher's
prior consent in any form of binding or cover other than that in
which it is published and without a similar condition including this
condition being imposed on the subsequent purchaser

JF

CITY OF COVENTRY
18·4·94
SCHOOLS
LIBRARY
SERVICE
JW
LIBRARIES

For Judith

AN ECHO is a very strange thing. It has a kind of life of its own. You call out in your real voice, and other voices come back to you, your own, and yet not your own, an answer from somewhere or someone else.

Kath has often gone over it in her mind, but she still cannot be sure what happened to her that autumn morning, at the end of her stay with Aunty Kitty and Uncle Stan. Whose voices were they that she heard? And who, listening, was she? Though in a kind of inside, underneath way she is, in fact, deeply sure. It is something she will never, ever forget.

It began with a letter. A little white envelope, addressed with small upright careful handwriting in blue biro to her mother.

'GOOD,' SAID her mother, putting the letter down beside her coffee mug. 'Aunty Kitty says "yes".'

Kath lowered her spoon. Suddenly she did not feel like eating the bowl of cereal in front of her. It had been her mother's idea that Kath should go and stay in the country for half-term. It would be fun, she'd said.

Kath said, 'But Aunty Kitty's *old*.'

'Oh, Kath. But you liked it when we called in on her, remember? I suppose that lot of kittens will be grown up and gone, but you never know, there might be more.'

7

'Ye-es,' said Kath.

It had been last autumn, a year ago. They had driven out for a picnic, high on the downs near Aunty Kitty's village, and then they'd called in on Aunty Kitty and Great-Uncle Stan.

'Just for a cup of tea,' her mother had said, as they crowded into the dark cottage, but there was a warm smell of baking and Aunty Kitty had made a cake. So they had sat out on a bench in the back garden and eaten it. Kath had played with Patch's kittens in the sun, and they had stayed on, and while her mother and Aunty Kitty had talked, Kath had climbed up the apple tree to pick the apples that Aunty Kitty couldn't reach. She and her father had filled three big boxes. One box had gone home with them in the boot of the car, and the crisp sweet little apples had lasted them right through October.

But Uncle Stan had stayed indoors; he was not very well, and had been a little grumpy.

'Do I have to go?' Kath now asked.

'But, Kath, you said you'd like to. I've already asked her, and she says she's clearing the little room at the back for you. Besides, what else am I to do with you while I'm away? You're not big enough to be here all by yourself while your father's out at work each day.'

Kath's mother was booked in to go up north for a short course. Kath had heard her talking about it, but hadn't paid much attention. It was something to do with her job; she was a Maths teacher at the big comprehensive.

'Only a week,' said her mother, 'that's not long. Well, a bit more, Friday to Sunday.'

8

'That's ages,' said Kath, counting on her fingers. 'That's ten days.'

'But she'll be glad of your help,' Kath's mother went on. 'Because her legs are bad, and I expect you can do the shopping for them.'

That would be nice, thought Kath, imagining herself walking down the lane to the village store with a basket over her arm. At home, they drove to the supermarket after school, and her mother was always in such a rush. There was no little corner shop near enough for Kath to go to on her own.

'Think of it as your good deed for the day – for all those days,' said her mother. 'Aunty Kitty says she'll be glad to get to know her great-niece better.'

'Is that what I am?' asked Kath, surprised. Of course. Aunty Kitty was really her great-aunt, but because her mother had always called her Aunty Kitty, they all did. 'How old is she?'

'I forget exactly,' said her mother. 'She was older than your gran. Seventy-eightyish? You can ask her when you get there. Now finish up or we'll be late for school.'

ALL THAT week Kath thought about all the things she must pack. Her anorak, for going to the shop, and her new shoes. Her mother made three lists; one for Kath, one for herself for her residential course, and one for Kath's father of things not to forget while they were both away.

Yet, as half-term drew nearer, Kath found herself walking about with a great lump of worry in the back of her mind. It was going to be very strange, sleeping away from home for the first time for such a long while all by herself. She wished she had never said yes.

WHEN THE day came, it was raining. Kath's mother picked her up early straight from school, and then drove all the way down the motorway with the wipers going at full speed. Every time they came up close behind a lorry, there was so much spray that Kath could hardly see anything at all, but after a while the rain stopped and the sun gleamed on the wet road. Kath was delighted to catch a sudden glimpse of rainbow in the fine mist thrown up by the car ahead. Maybe it was a good sign.

They turned off, up a smaller road, and the downs opened wide on either side, rolling away into the distance. A tractor was ploughing, with a crowd of

seagulls rising and falling and settling behind it, their white wings sharp against the wet brown earth. The road stretched ahead, a long grey ruler, until far off on the right Kath saw a signpost. Nearer, and she could read the name of Aunty Kitty's village. Down the right-hand road they went, keeping to the outer rim of a deep-wooded coomb, and then another right turn and they were plunging down a high-banked lane, roofed over with yellow leaves.

On down, past several gateways, and then her mother braked and drove the car on to a steeply sloping patch of grass. They had arrived.

Through the car window Kath was looking up at the gable end of the long low cottage, and as soon as the car engine stopped, she could hear church bells ringing. Her mother walked up a narrow path along the front of the cottage to the door, and Aunty Kitty

came out in her yellow overall. 'Ah, there you are, my dears, come you in.'

Kath lifted her bag off the back seat and followed her mother along the path and into the dark stair-well by the front door. Aunty Kitty padded ahead of them in her slippers to the kitchen.

'Now, you shall have a cup of tea afore you go back,' she said, putting the big flat-bottomed kettle on the Rayburn stove. 'Stan's better, I'm glad to say, or I don' know what I'd do.'

Kath stood uncertainly in the middle of the room, unsure where to go. There was no sign of Patch. From here the church bells were even louder, and out of the back window she could see the tower through the trees. 'Why are they ringing the bells?' she asked. 'It's not Sunday.'

''Tis practice night,' said Aunty Kitty. 'And there's a weddin' tomorrow, they'll be ringin' till all hours, I dare say. I don' hear 'em so dratted loud now, my hearin's not what 'twas. 'Tis an ill wind that blows nobody any good.' She chuckled, her face crinkling up, like one of her little rosy apples, thought Kath.

Kath sat down in a corner, holding her steaming cup of tea. While Aunty Kitty and her mother talked, she counted the bells, clanging one, two, three, down the scale to eight, over and over, until the rhythm failed and there was a pause, and then a jangle of what sounded like two or three together. *One . . . twothreefour . . . five, six . . . seveneight.* Again they rang and again muddled, and then the third time they recovered the beat and went down evenly. Then began a new tune, *up down up down,*

down up down down, which they played again, and then again. Kath lost count.

Her mother put down her cup and stood up to go. She gave Kath a quick hug, and·before Kath had time to say anything, she was out through the door and into the seat of the car. The door slammed, the engine started, the car backed down off the grass into the lane and she was gone.

To Kath's surprise, Aunty Kitty put an arm round her and gave her a squeeze. 'There now, child. Come, I'll show you your room.' She turned and climbed the stairs, Kath following.

At the top of the stairs there was a tiny landing, and then Aunty Kitty opened the door into a small room with a low sloping ceiling. There was a tunnel through the slope, and at the far end of it a little window, at just about Kath's waist level, through which she could see the church tower. She leant on the sill, and found she could look down on the apple tree and the back garden, and the rest of the village roofs, jumbling down in thatch and tile and slate towards the church.

'Here's your bed,' said Aunty Kitty. 'And you can put your things in there. We'll have a proper look at the village tomorrow, maybe go and watch the weddin' and see all the folks dressed up. You come down when you're ready and we'll have a bite to eat afore you go to bed.'

KATH WOKE early the next morning. There was a scratching sound by the window, and a miaow. Kath swung her feet out of bed and saw Patch's face,

13

looking in through the glass. She opened the window and let the cat in. Then she pulled the door wide on to the landing, but Patch followed her back to bed, and when Kath huddled down again under the eiderdown, Patch pushed her nose under it and curled up against her, purring loudly.

Kath lay in bed and waited until she heard the church clock strike eight, and then she got up and dressed. She could hear a loud rattling sound coming from below, and then Aunty Kitty moving about. Patch ran down the stairs ahead of her. There was no sign of Uncle Stan, but Aunty Kitty was riddling the Rayburn, peering into it and picking out the clinkers, which she dropped into a bucket full of ash.

She turned her head when Kath came in. 'Oh, that wicked Patch,' she said fondly. 'Did she spend the night in your room? What do you have for breakfast at home?'

Kath couldn't see any of the cereals she was used to. There was a teapot on the table by the window, some toast, butter, and a small carton of long-life milk. She decided she had better fit in. 'We have toast, and tea.'

Aunty Kitty reached down plates and cups and saucers, and laid for three. She left the room and climbed the stairs with a cup of tea in her hand. Kath sat at the table and waited for her to come back. Patch leapt on to Kath's knee and pushed her face against her hand, and then climbed on to the table towards the butter. Hastily Kath lifted her off.

She wondered whether to begin on the toast or not. Aunty Kitty was being ages. After a while she

15

took a piece, and was just starting to spread it with butter when Aunty Kitty reappeared.

She was shaking her head, talking to herself. 'I don' like it, I don' like it at all –' She stopped, as if seeing Kath for the first time.

'Your Uncle Stan's not so good this mornin',' she said. 'But don' you worry, he'll be right as rain by lunchtime and I'll take you down the village.' She sat down at the table and poured the tea.

'I could go by myself,' said Kath. 'I could go to the shops for you this morning.'

Aunty Kitty spread a piece of toast and frowned. 'No, 'tis not safe for a child. The lane is that narrow there's no pavement, and all them buses and lorries go down it ever so fast. I couldn't let you.'

'Oh,' said Kath.

Aunty Kitty said, 'I mind a long time back, when I was a girl, I was near run into comin' up the lane. An' that were only Chalky White on 'is butcher's round, tearin' down on 'is bike. 'Twas lucky no one was hurt bad. But that Chalky, he were always tearin' about, always helter-skelter.' Aunty Kitty glared at Kath. 'An' they will still do it,' she went on, 'all on 'em jus' the same. They never learn. One of these days there'll be an accident. 'Twouldn't be so bad if they was only takin' risks theirselves, but 'tis others as will be hurt.' She shook her head.

Kath sat in silence. So much for her good deeds. She waited while Aunty Kitty ate, and then pushed back her chair and stood up, beginning to clear away her plate.

'Don't scrape your chair like that,' said Aunty Kitty sharply. 'Your Uncle Stan is sleepin' upstairs,

least I hope he is. He had a bad night.' She rose and took the plate and cup out of Kath's hands. 'I'll do that, we can't have anything broken.'

Kath gulped. She didn't seem to be able to do anything right. She stood up feeling helpless, while Aunty Kitty bustled about clearing up the breakfast things, putting down a saucer of milk for Patch.

Kath watched Patch's pink tongue flick up the milk. 'Will she have more kittens soon?'

Aunty Kitty swung round from the sink. 'She's gettin' on a bit for havin' kits all the time. She's an old lady, same as me.'

'Aunty Kitty, how old are you?'

Aunty Kitty pursed her lips. 'That's not summat as you should go around askin', didn't your mother tell you?'

Kath shook her head, unable to speak. Desperately she wanted, more than anything in the world, to be back in the kitchen at home.

She bent down to stroke Patch, smoothing the thick fur with her fingers and running her hand up the plumy tail. Patch flicked her tail and came back for more. Then she stalked out through the back door.

LATER THAT morning, when Kath was in the back garden, wondering what to do with herself, she heard a ring at the front door. Through the kitchen window she saw Aunty Kitty go to answer it and, curious, Kath followed to see who it might be.

A lady stood there, holding a tray of poppies and a can. Aunty Kitty went upstairs for money.

'Hello,' said the lady. 'I've not seen you here before. Who are you?'

'I'm Kath. Staying with Aunty Kitty and Uncle Stan.'

'Ah. You'll be Ruth's daughter, from London.'

'That's right,' said Kath, surprised. 'How did you know?'

'Your aunty has told the whole village, that's how. She were that pleased that you was comin'. She didn' have no children of her own, you know, and she's ever so proud of your mum. It's Ruth this, an' Ruth that, all day long.'

Kath was astonished. Then why had Aunty Kitty been so short with her?

The lady picked out a poppy and pinned it to Kath's jumper. 'There y'are, are real pretty one. You can wear it to church next week, on Remembrance Sunday.'

Aunty Kitty came back with the money and took two more poppies. 'I'm sorry to keep you waitin'. 'Tis Stan. He's took bad with 'is chest, an' I'm that bothered, I don't know whether I'm comin' or goin'.'

'Don't you worry, he'll be back on his feet in no time,' said the lady.

She went down the path, but half-way along she turned and waved to Kath. 'Give my best to your mum. Elsie Jarvis, that's my name. She'll remember me.'

Aunty Kitty went back into the kitchen. She poured water into a bowl, filled it with potatoes and sat down at the table to peel them. 'Not much older than you I was, when the armistice were signed,'

19

she said. 'An' your gran were five. I remember it like yesterday. We was in school, not where it is now, by the main road, but the old school, where them railings is, jus' down from the church. An' Miss Sawbridge come runnin' into the room, wavin' her arms an' shoutin' "Armistice, armistice!"'

'What's armistice?'

''Twas the end of the war, the Great War. Not the one that your Uncle Stan fought in, against Hitler. No. A long way back. 1914 it began. An' 1918 it ended. There was so many went, so many. All the lads from the village, all the men from the camp. An' so many never come back.'

She sighed, a deep shuddering sigh. The half-peeled potato fell from her hand back into the water with a small plop, but she seemed not to notice. She was a long way away, her small face drooped and crumpled, all the bustle gone out of her. There was a moment's silence, then she wiped the back of her hand across her eyes. 'There now,' she said, brisk again. 'Too much thinkin' back, that'll never do.'

She finished the potato, slipped it into the pan and put on the lid. Then she pushed back her chair and stood up. 'Come on, Kath, we'll go up an' make your bed.'

UNCLE STAN was not better by lunchtime. He stayed in his room and Aunty Kitty took trays of food up to him. All Kath knew of the wedding was the run-away gallop of bells sounding through the trees, and a glimpse of two cars going down the lane with people in hats.

Later that evening in her bedroom, Kath was startled by a series of bangs. Jumping out of bed, she went to the window and saw a rocket shoot skyward, exploding in a scatter of stars. Of course, it was bonfire night. For a while she pressed her face to the glass, hoping for more, but although she heard them, no more rockets crossed the bit of sky that she could see. They must have been coming from some other part of the village.

She gave up and went back to bed, thinking longingly of other years and parties with friends. Huddled under the bedclothes, she read most of the book that her mother had put in her bag, before switching out the light and going to sleep.

It was Monday before Aunty Kitty was ready to go down the village.

Kath ran upstairs to put on her anorak and new shoes, but when she came down again, she saw that Aunty Kitty still had on her yellow overall, and her swollen feet were pushed into slippers. She had put a cardigan over the overall.

'I don' feel the cold, never have,' she said. They set off down the road, Kath carrying the basket.

At the foot of the lane was a bus shelter, and hanging about it were three boys, much older than Kath, while a fourth sat astride his bike, swinging the front wheel idly from side to side. They were laughing, but as soon as they saw Aunty Kitty, the laughter snapped off like a light.

'Don' know what to do with theirselves, gurt great lummocks,' huffed Aunty Kitty. 'Now if they

was mine, I'd soon tan their backsides, give 'em summat to think about. 'Tis the parents' fault, that's what I always say.'

Kath didn't like to ask what Aunty Kitty thought the boys ought to be doing. After all, it was half-term.

In front of the bus shelter was the village green. It was unlike any other village green that Kath had ever seen, an odd gap among all the tightly crammed cottages and gardens. It was in a kind of hollow, though the grass was level enough, and there were houses along only one side of it. The top end was made by the lane where the bus shelter was, and it sloped away downhill towards a gate and woods at the far end. All along one side was a high bank, overgrown with trees and tangled with brambles, and along the other, opposite, were some cottages, the village store and a pub. Outside the pub swung a sign, painted with a green tree, and the words the Oak Tree. Kath looked, but there was no tree anywhere near it.

'Why is it called that?'

'Huh!' said Aunty Kitty. 'There was a big oak, bin there as long as anyone could remember, but when they made the pavement, they put it right up to the trunk. Tarmacked it up. It couldn't get no water, see. An' it died. They had to cut it down.'

They turned down past the Oak Tree and went into the village shop. It was a post office as well, Kath noticed, looking round. Kath's mother had given her some money, and she fingered the coins happily in her anorak pocket.

Aunty Kitty went up to the counter and asked for

some tins, bread, biscuits, butter and long-life milk.

'Why don't you get it fresh from the milkman?' asked Kath, putting the carton into the basket.

''Twould be taken from our door,' said Aunty Kitty. 'I told the milkman, I'm not orderin' milk from you to have it taken by the likes o' them,' and she jerked a thumb over her shoulder towards the bus stop.

Once more, Kath was surprised. At home the milk was delivered long before anyone was up, and as far as she knew, it had never gone missing. Could there be more things stolen in Aunty Kitty's village than in London? Kath bit her lip and turned her face away to study the tray of chocolate bars and sweets on top of the counter. 'Can I buy some?'

''Tis a waste of money, but if you're set on it, I suppose I can't stop you,' said Aunty Kitty. 'When we was your age, there weren't no money to spare for sweets.'

All the joy of choosing vanished with Aunty Kitty's words. The shop lady gave Aunty Kitty an angry look and said to Kath, 'There now, you choose one you'd like and it can be yours for nothing.'

Kath looked up gratefully. No one in a London shop had ever said that to her. This village was full of surprises. Aunty Kitty gave a snort, and walked towards the door. Kath was finding it impossible to decide between a Mars bar and another kind, and behind her she heard the door open and then slam. She swung round and saw that Aunty Kitty was outside in the road.

'You don' want to mind your aunty,' said the

shop lady. 'She don' mean to be unkind, she just don' know about children. Here, you have this one,' and she pressed the Mars bar into Kath's hand.

Kath hurried out of the shop. Aunty Kitty was already stumping up the lane, a small determined figure, white hair bobbing up and down. Kath ran after her. The three boys skateboarded down the hill towards her, passing Aunty Kitty with great wide exaggerated swoops, shouting and hallooing. It looked fun, and Kath envied them their game. The one with the bicycle followed them down, ringing his bell as hard as he could. Kath found it difficult to see them as hardened thieves.

KATH LAY in bed that night and looked at the ceiling. Yellow flowers marched in lines down the slope over her head. If she half closed her eyes, she could make a diagonal pattern as well. She shut them, and counted off the days. Friday, Saturday, Sunday, Monday. She had been there four days, not even half-way yet, and it seemed like for ever.

Tomorrow she would ask Aunty Kitty if they might telephone home from the call-box in the lane. Her father would not be back from work until after six, after dark, but perhaps Aunty Kitty would help. She turned out the light and curled up under the eiderdown, pulling it up cosy round her chin, but it was a long time before she could sleep. The quiet and the dark pressed in on her.

The only sound to break the silence was the hum of an approaching car up the lane. Briefly the wall by the window was alight; white bars wheeled across the ceiling, faded, and were gone. The car's engine grew fainter and vanished into the night.

NEXT MORNING sunlight slanted into the little kitchen. Aunty Kitty flung wide open the window, and Uncle Stan was down for breakfast for the first time since Kath's arrival.

'Well now, young Kathie,' he said. 'What would you like to be doin' today? I'm goin' up Pearce's, up the top road, to make sure Frank's all right for Sunday and the parade. You can come along if you'd like.'

'Yes, please,' said Kath.

Aunty Kitty said, 'Are you sure you're all right to go out, Stan?'

'Course I am,' said Uncle Stan. 'Anyway, Kathie'll look after me, won't you?' and he winked across the table.

'Yes,' said Kath, delighted.

They set off up the lane after breakfast, leaving Aunty Kitty busying round the kitchen. Uncle Stan walked with a stick, and Kath had to slow down and wait for him. Over their heads the roof of branches was almost bare against a sky of high, racing clouds. A cold wind blew scurries of dead leaves down towards them, and heaped them up against the bank.

At the top of the lane Uncle Stan halted, panting slightly, and waved his stick towards a stone cross which stood on the grass verge. 'You see that? Just put that up, they have. 'Tis a war memorial. There'll be a procession. After church. This Sunday. You'll see. With a band an' all.'

'Who'll be in it?'

'Ah. I shall, an' Frank. And there's others. We wear our medals, see.'

28

Kath was impressed. 'Have you won a medal?'

He laughed. 'Not that special,' he said. 'Just to show we was in the war, and which campaigns – which bit we was in.'

'Will there be anyone from the armistice war?'

He shook his head. 'There's none of 'em left. Not as is well enough to march. There's only old Chalky White from Bishop's Farm, an' he's ninety an' some if he's a day, an' his mind's wanderin' a bit these days, I'm told. Mebbe someone'll bring him along, he oughter see it.' He shook his head, thoughtful.

They walked along the top road in silence. Past several gateways, they came to Frank's house. Frank was outside, sawing wood, but he stopped when Uncle Stan called to him, and his red face broke into a smile. He came to the gate and

clapped Uncle Stan on the back.

'Good to see yer,' he said. 'All right then for Sunday?'

Uncle Stan said, 'This is young Kathie, from London,' and Kath found herself shaking hands.

The two men talked about the arrangements for the parade. Kath stood waiting for them to finish, listening but not really listening. Uncle Stan was saying that Chalky White ought to see the dedication. Frank said, 'But Chalky White 'asn't bin on a parade since I bin in the village. Far as I knows, 'e won't come on 'em.'

Uncle Stan said, 'But he oughter be *told* about the dedication. This is different. 'Tis the new cross. And 'tis for 'is regiment.'

Kath shifted from foot to foot, and Frank looked down at her. 'In jus' a minute,' he said, 'I got summat as you would like to see. Jus' you bide there,' and he turned back to Uncle Stan. 'Mebbe you're right. I leaves it to you. 'E oughter be there.' Then he said to Kath, 'Now you come along with me.'

He led the way round to the back of the house. On one side of the back yard were three rabbit hutches. Two were empty, but in the third was a big black and white rabbit, nibbling a cabbage leaf. He cocked up one ear when he saw them coming, and then scratched behind it with one leg.

Frank disappeared into the house and came back with a carrot, and showed Kath how to hold it through the wire netting, so that she could watch the rabbit scrunch it up inch by inch. When there was not much carrot left between the rabbit's teeth and her fingers, she let it go with a squeal, and both men laughed.

· On the way home along the top road, Kath and Uncle Stan crossed over and walked on the far side. Kath noticed another pub, this one called the Patriot's Arms. Tucked away behind it she could see grass, and wooden chairs and tables, and a wide spreading tree with branches almost touching the ground.

There must be so many hidden corners in the village that she had not had a chance to explore. She had never seen a tree so crying out to be climbed. She pulled Uncle Stan's hand to bring him to a halt.

'Can I go and climb that tree?'

'That's a good idea,' said Uncle Stan. 'In we go.' He looked up and down the road, but there was no one in sight. 'I'll jus' have a pint, but not a word to Aunty Kitty, mind,' and he gave her another wink.

THAT EVENING Kath watched the children's programmes that Aunty Kitty had switched on for her in the front room. When Uncle Stan came in for the news, and lowered himself with a grunt into his chair, she went to look for her aunt. She found her at the table in the kitchen, with a cup of tea in front of her and Patch curled up on her lap.

'Do you think we could phone home? I want to know how Mum and Dad are getting on.'

Aunty Kitty looked blank. 'What's that?'

Kath repeated her question.

Aunty Kitty said, 'I didn't hear you right first time. Oh, Kath love, I've jus' this minute sat down, an' my legs is that bad. If I give you the money, can you do it yourself? 'Tis no distance to the call-box, 'tis just down the lane, an' there's a light in there.'

Kath took a deep breath. She mustn't be a nuisance, she thought, so she said yes, she was sure she could manage. Inside cold panic rose, but it was too late. She heard Aunty Kitty telling her where to find the money, found herself passing the purse over to her and then accepting the proffered loose change. She did not confess that the only phone she had ever used was the one on the table by the sofa at home.

She put on her anorak and opened the front door and went out into the night. The morning's cold wind had dropped, but the sky was blanketed with cloud, and there was not a star to be seen. The lamp further down the lane made a glare of yellow light, and beyond it she could see the bright rectangle of the call-box, but all the rest was black dark. The banks of the lane loomed up on either side.

Kath pulled up the collar of her anorak, pushed her hands into the pockets and ran down to the call-box, looking neither to right nor to left.

She hauled open the door with both hands and squashed herself in through the gap. Two or three cigarette butts lay in a pool of water on the floor, and a four-letter word was scratched across the metal facing her. There was a smell of smoke.

She stood on tiptoe and studied the instructions, the change clutched tight in one hand. *Lift handset*, it said. She took the bright blue receiver off the hook, and at once words flashed across the tiny screen

level with her eyes, *Minimum charge 10p*. She fumbled for a ten-pence piece, found one, and put it in.

Dial number said the instructions. She spelt out her home number on the little buttons, waiting for the ringing tone. There was a high-pitched buzz. Alarmed, she put back the receiver, wondering what she had done wrong, and heard the ten-pence piece tumble down inside. She looked again at the instructions, but wherever she stood, the bottom half was hidden behind the phone fitting; she was too short to see over it.

The inside of the call-box blurred over and she felt the sharp sting of tears. She fought them back, wiping her eyes with the back of her sleeve, and

tried to find a second ten-pence piece. There wasn't one. By now it was no good, tears were running down her face.

There was a sudden banging on the glass behind her. She started and swung round. A white face was looking at her, and a large knuckly hand was rapping on the window-pane.

The face was saying something, mouthing words at her. Kath could not understand them, she stood helpless, trapped, and then, before she could do anything, the door opened. The man came into the call-box.

Kath pressed herself against the wall. There was no way she could escape. She stared at him in terror.

And then it came to her. It was not a strange man, it was the largest of the boys from the bus stop, one of the skateboarding trio. He was repeating what he had said, and put a hand on her arm. Kath gave a frightened yelp.

When he said the words a third time, they rearranged themselves in Kath's mind with a meaning, and it dawned on her that he was offering help. 'I said can't yer work that thing?' he said patiently.

Kath gulped. She felt ashamed. 'I can't reach,' she said. 'I can't see what it says to do, and I've used the 10p now.'

He said, 'It's OK, don't be so scared. I'll do it for yer. Tryin' to get yer mum, was you?'

'No, my dad.'

'What's yer number?' he asked. 'Give me the money. You'll be needin' more 'n 10p.'

Kath handed over the remaining coins, repeating her number.

'But you don' live round 'ere,' he said. 'You got to do the bit fer – where d'yer come from?'

'London,' said Kath.

Slowly he checked the big dialling-list and found the two codes for London. 'You got to do that first,' he said, 'and *then* yer number. Which one are you, inner or outer?'

Kath looked at him helplessly. 'I'm not sure.'

'Is it 081?' he asked.

She was silent.

'I'll give it a go,' he said, 'an' if it's wrong, we'll try the other.'

Frowning, he fed in more money and pressed the buttons, holding the blue receiver to his ear. There was a short pause, and then his face cleared and he handed it over to Kath. She could hear her father's voice coming out of it, 'Hello, hello, who is that?'

'It's me, Kath. How – has Mum rung you?'

'I've written you a letter, Kath. Yes, she's fine, I spoke to her last night. I was wondering how you were getting on. Are you OK?'

Relief flooded through her, it was so wonderful to hear his voice; the nightmares vanished. 'I'm all right.'

'You don't sound all right. Are you sure?'

'Yes, yes, really.'

The boy patted her shoulder, and twisted himself out through the door. She listened while her father talked, telling her that her mother had hardly had a spare minute, that they were working them very hard, from the time they got up till ten at night, that she had found it hard to snatch the time for a phone call, but that she was enjoying it.

'Goodbye, Kath,' he said. 'Send me a postcard. Give my love to Aunty Kitty and Uncle Stan. Be good,' and he rang off.

Kath put back the receiver and opened the door. She stepped out into the lane, looking for the boy to thank him, but she could not see him. She began the climb up the hill towards the cottage, and as she passed the yellow street-light, there was an approaching rumble of wheels and the boy swung down towards her on his skateboard.

'Thank you,' she shouted as he looped past her.

'That's all right,' the words flowed back over his shoulder, as he went on down and out of sight towards the darkening Green.

'ALL RIGHT then?' said Aunty Kitty, when Kath came back in through the front door.

'Yes,' said Kath. 'What's he called, that big boy with the skateboard?'

'Oh my, did they go botherin' you? I should 'a come. Always hangin' about the call-box and the bus stop, they are, an' goin' down the lane on them board things, an' after dark too. 'Tis dangerous for other folks. I've a mind to say summat to the Parish Council about 'em. An' that tall one, Kevin White, he's the worst on 'em, he is. There's no good in them Whites, the village would be better off without 'em.'

Uncle Stan came into the kitchen. 'Hush up, Kitty. They don' mean no harm. We was all boys once. An' that reminds me, someone had better go and see Chalky White about Sunday. Well, young Kathie, and how's yer mum?'

Kath smiled at him gratefully, and recounted the report from her father. But she said nothing about Kevin's part in the phone call.

THE BRIDLE-PATH to Bishop's Farm and Chalky White's cottage continued straight on from where the lane ended, up by the new memorial, cutting across the high plateau of the downs. The wind came roaring out of the south-west with only an occasional thorn-hedge or hunched-over stand of beeches to hinder it.

Kath had never seen so much sky, nor such long tattered streamers of cloud. She could see from horizon to horizon on all sides. I am a small open

boat on the sea, she thought, for so it was, a wide rolling sea of grass with a huge swell running, lifting rounded billows of greenness, falling into dips of lighter chalk where the ground was ploughed. She wished she had brought a thicker coat. She was having to walk slowly because of Uncle Stan, and the fingers of her right hand were going dead with cold.

Uncle Stan was walking with dogged determination, but his breath was coming in gasps, and he obviously had none to spare for speech.

They came to a lane marked Ladysmith Road, and then a sign to The Camp. Uncle Stan stopped for a rest, and waved his stick towards the lane. 'Used to be a gurt big camp down there. All the soldiers used to be there.'

Kath followed the direction of his stick. There was a wide ploughed field and, as she watched, a flock of black and white birds rose up with shrill cries and wheeled overhead, dipping sideways to ride the wind on blunt wings. They dropped to earth again further away.

'Peewits,' said Uncle Stan.

All that seemed to be left of the camp was a couple of cottages beyond the field, and then two or three huts.

'Was that for the armistice war?' she asked.

'Both wars,' said Uncle Stan. 'To begin with for the First World War. They trained 'em hereabouts, and then they'd go off in the troop trains for Belgium and France, to Southampton and that, and then again in the Second World War. That's why the pub where you climbed the tree is called the Patriot's Arms.'

He rose to his feet and began to walk forward again along the bridle-path. Kath followed after him. 'Were you there? In the camp?'

Uncle Stan nodded. 'Hush up for now, Kathie. I gotta save me breath. We gotta get to Chalky's cottage.'

They walked on into the wind for some time without talking. At last the farm and barns came into view, and beyond them, hull down in a sea of overgrown garden, a pair of red-brick cottages.

Uncle Stan went up to the smaller of the two cottages and rapped on the door with his stick.

'Who's there?' came from inside.

They opened the door and went in. An old man

with thick white hair was sitting in an armchair by the fireside, with a blanket over his knees. Coals glowed, banked up in the grate, and Kath crouched in front of them to warm her hands, while Uncle Stan spoke to the old man.

Chalky was nodding his head. 'That's right, you get warm. I don' see too many folk from the village these days. I'd make you a cup of tea if my durn legs wasn't so shaky.'

Uncle Stan said, 'Don' worry, Chalky. We can get one ourselves. I 'spect you'd like one as well. In a minute. But we didn' come fer that, we come about the parade.'

Chalky's hand plucked anxiously at the blanket over his knees, and he turned a puzzled face up towards Uncle Stan. 'Whassat? I don' know nothin' 'bout that. Parade?'

Kath watched the long fingers making little shaky pulling movements at the wool. Chalky's knuckles were knobbly and reddened, and there were brown patches on the backs of his hands, but his skin had a transparent pink and white delicacy she had not seen before. Perhaps it was because he was very old. She looked at his face and decided that he looked nice. It was a good face, a dignified face, with a long straight nose and darting blue eyes.

Suddenly the eyes met hers, and the old man smiled, his whole face alight. 'Kitty!' he said. 'I never thought to see you again.' He put out a hand and took hers, drawing her towards him.

'No,' said Uncle Stan. ' 'Tis not Kitty. 'Tis Ruth's daughter, Kath.'

44

The old man peered into Kath's face. 'But I could 'a sworn . . . Not Kitty?' He looked disappointed.

Kath felt herself flush deep crimson, and she pulled back.

'I know I do get things all mingled up,' said Chalky. 'But you're Kitty to the life . . .' He shook his head slowly as if he was unwilling to believe that she was not. Then he let go of her hand.

'You was thinkin' from a long time back,' said Uncle Stan. 'From when Kitty were little more 'n a child.'

Kath was embarrassed. She did not know what to say. She turned towards the mantelpiece because Chalky was still staring at her, and fixed her eyes on the ornaments. There was a brown faded photo of a young man in army uniform. Serious face. Straight nose. No twinkle in the eyes, which looked gravely into the camera lens.

Chalky saw what she was looking at. 'Ay,' he said, 'that were me, afore I went off to the trenches. I were that keen to go, I couldn't 'ardly wait. By the time it were all over, there was that many killed, there wasn't a family in the village save ours but 'ad lost a son or a father or a brother. I were lucky, I come through. But a lot of me mates didn't.'

He paused, and put his head in his hands. 'And she never did forgive me,' he said. There was a long silence. Then 'I tries not to think of it. I 'aven't for years, but jus' lately it's bin comin' back, stronger 'n ever. I 'ears the guns. The noise o' them guns. Like thunder, all the time. Never lettin' up. An' I'm back in the mud an' the wet. An' there's Tom, dead beside me.'

Neither Uncle Stan nor Kath spoke. The old man looked into Kath's eyes, and said with sudden force, banging his fist down on his knee, 'Don' you ever let 'em tell you there's glory in war. I seen it. I know. You take my word fer it, 'tis all waste. All them dead. A right bloody mess them generals made of it.'

'Hush up, Chalky,' said Uncle Stan. 'She's only a child. You shouldn' talk like that in front of her.'

'All the more reason,' said Chalky. ''Tis 'er and 'er lot as will 'ave ter get it right. We didn't.'

Uncle Stan said, 'That's as may be. But what we come about was the dedication of the new war memorial at the top of Pearce's, an' the Remembrance Sunday parade. 'Tis this Sunday, after mornin' church. I know you're not much of a one fer church, but I reckoned you'd not want to miss seein' the dedication.'

The old man scowled. 'I 'aven't got much time fer parades an' that,' he said. 'Best memorial, 'twould be not to let it 'appen again. Paradin' about, 'tis games fer the livin', 'twon' bring back the dead.'

Uncle Stan said patiently, 'I'm not askin' yer to parade. I'm askin' yer to come an' see the cross dedicated. It's fer Tom an' all of 'em. Vince too. All yer mates.'

'Nobody asked me,' said Chalky. 'What do they want to go an' put it there for? It should 'a bin down on the Green, that's where we all went from.'

'Chalky, you always was a cussed varmint,' said Uncle Stan. 'All right, I shall tell everybody that you didn' want to be there.'

'Now wait a minute. Hold on,' said Chalky, and

his whole body began to tremble. He leant forward and put a hand on Uncle Stan's arm, gripping it with long fingers. 'I didn' say I didn' want to be there.'

'Now yer talkin',' said Uncle Stan. 'But how're we goin' ter get yer there? Can yer get a lift with Ken an' them from the farm?'

That would be the farmer and his wife, Kath thought. They kept an eye on Chalky, Uncle Stan had said so.

'I don' like to bother 'em, see,' said Chalky. 'They got enough to do fer me without that.'

'Well, what about the rest of them Whites?' said Uncle Stan. 'What about yer grandson, Bob, an' Margaret, an' all them kids they got. For goodness' sakes, there's enough o' them. What about young Kevin?'

'Well now, there's a thought. Bob an' Margaret, 'tis no good askin' them, but young Kevin now. He could mebbe 'elp get me there. 'E's a big lad. 'E's not seventeen yet, but 'e can drive, 'e's driven the farm tractor more 'n once in the field when they was gettin' in the harvest this summer. I knows fer a fact.'

'I'll send 'im up to talk to yer,' said Uncle Stan. 'An' I shall expect to see yer there. Now Kathie, put the kettle on, that's a good girl.'

KATH'S LETTER from her father lay on her plate next morning. It said little that he had not already told her in their telephone conversation, but she remembered that she had promised to send a postcard home. There was still time. She asked

Aunty Kitty if she had one.

'I'm afraid I don',' said Aunty Kitty.

Uncle Stan said, 'We can walk down to the shop later, Kathie. I was going anyway.'

'What you want to go there for, Stan?' asked Aunty Kitty sharply. 'You're not set on gettin' more cigarettes, I hope.'

'Well, I wasn't,' said Uncle Stan mischievously. 'But now you mentions it, I jus' might.'

Aunty Kitty frowned, but then, realizing she was being teased, smiled unwillingly.

Uncle Stan and Kath set out for the shop as soon as Kath had fetched her anorak. The lane was deserted, but Kath could hear shouts and the thud of a football coming up from the hollow.

As they passed the bus stop, there was a yell, 'Yer stupid idiot!' and the ball soared over their heads and landed higher up the road. It bounced against the bank, came to rest and then rolled slowly back down the hill towards them. With a quick glance to make sure it was safe to do so, Kath ran to pick up the ball.

'Look out for cars,' shouted Uncle Stan.

Kath hurried back with the ball in her arms. Two boys were running up towards them, jostling each other good-naturedly. There weren't any cars. If Uncle Stan and Aunty Kitty thought the lane was dangerous from traffic, they should try the roads she was used to crossing at home.

She could see the rest of the players now, standing watching on the Green, four or five more boys. Two she thought she recognized, but Kevin White was not among them. Uncle Stan took the ball from her, and lobbed it over the approaching boys' heads down on to the grass.

'You want to keep it off the road,' he shouted.

'Cheers,' said the boys. 'Thanks.'

'An' if you see Kevin White,' said Uncle Stan, 'tell 'im I've got a little job for 'im.'

One of the boys, now running after the ball, acknowledged the message with a raised thumb. Kath stood to watch as they charged in a swift-moving pack to the far end of the Green, their worn trainers skidding on the muddy grass. The ball moved in quick zigzags from one to the other, and even without knowing much about the game, she could see that they were good.

Reluctantly she followed Uncle Stan into the shop. There was no problem about choosing a postcard; there was only one which showed the village.

'Write it now,' said Uncle Stan, showing her the

shelf beside the post-office counter where there was a pen on a piece of string. 'I'll get a stamp. We'll make sure it gets there afore you do.'

KATH SAT in the church, waiting for the service to begin. The bells had been ringing high overhead from the tower as they walked from the cottage, a straight peal down the scale, loud and clear, followed by an echoing peal, fainter, muffled. And then the same again. Loud and then muffled, over and over. Kath wondered how they did it. She could still hear it, but not so deafening now she was inside. There was that special church smell of damp stone; she remembered it from the time they'd visited Bath Abbey.

On one side of her was Aunty Kitty. Kath looked at her. For the first time since Kath's arrival, Aunty Kitty was not wearing her yellow overall. She had

on a felt hat with a brim, and a coat, and her feet were pushed into shoes, but they must have been hurting her, because it had taken a long time to walk down past the Green and up the hill to the church.

On the other was Uncle Stan, his war medals pinned across his chest. He shifted his glasses up his nose and studied the hymn book, finding the place for Kath, and handing the book to her. Hymn 165, 'Oh God, Our Help in Ages Past'.

Kath put the book down open on the shelf in front of her and looked about. There were a great many people. How would she know what to do? At home they hardly ever went to church, except on Christmas Day, and then she was usually too excited about the pile of unopened presents waiting back home under the tree to pay much attention to the service. She liked singing the carols though.

Kath picked up the hymn book and read through the verses.

> Time, like an ever-rolling stream,
>   Bears all its sons away.
> They fly forgotten, as a dream
>   Dies at the opening day.

A funny hymn for Remembrance Sunday, she thought. Aren't we supposed to be remembering everyone who died, making sure they're *not* forgotten? She shut the book and gazed around.

There was an awful lot of waiting when you were with Aunty Kitty and Uncle Stan. Her mother would have arrived in the nick of time, panting in just before the service began. Or even tiptoeing in late, with people turning round to stare. Kath had

been deeply embarrassed on more than one occasion, at school and elsewhere, but now saw that it was a way of doing things that had its uses. It meant no waiting.

On the wall by the door there was a stone plaque with a list of names. Kath counted. Thirty-two names altogether, twenty-three under 1914–18, nine under 1939–45. The village used to be much smaller, Aunty Kitty had told her. When she'd been at the school, it had had only two classes and two teachers. Surely twenty-three was a great many?

She began to read down: *George Ashley, Henry Cook, Sydney Drake, Arthur Hicks, Reginald Johnson, Thomas Poulshott, Vincent Poulshott* – hang on. Thomas Poulshott, Vincent Poulshott. Hadn't Poulshott been her grandmother's name? Before she married? And Aunty Kitty's name? Then who were Thomas and Vincent? Brothers. Brothers of Aunty Kitty and her gran?

Kath swung round and took a quick look at Aunty Kitty, a side view under the felt hat. She could not ask. Not here, not now. The parson and the choir were coming down the side aisle from the vestry, the service was beginning. Everyone stood up.

Kath stood up, too, but swivelled round to look at the plaque again. There were no Whites. But then there wouldn't be. Chalky had said, *He'd been lucky, he'd come through*. Was that why Aunty Kitty was so bitter about the Whites? Not one of them gone, although there were so many of them, and her only two brothers killed? It wasn't possible for anything that was such long-gone history to go on mattering, was it? She remembered Aunty Kitty stumping up

the lane, so cross and determined, past Kevin White. Oh yes it was. It was, for somebody like Aunty Kitty.

And there's Tom, dead beside me, Chalky had said. Thomas Poulshott. Poor Chalky, all he'd done wrong in Aunty Kitty's eyes was to come home unharmed, leaving Tom dead on the battlefield.

All about her Kath heard the shifting and shuffling of the congregation, and realized with a start that she was head and shoulders above them, that most of them had knelt down. Hastily she turned to face the altar and knelt too, screwing up her eyes and putting her hands over her face, hoping that no one would notice that she did not know the words of the prayer.

She did better on the hymns, knowing the tunes from school. The service went surprisingly quickly, nothing like as long, it seemed to her, as the Christmas morning one at home.

The parson told everybody that the dedication would take place immediately after church, and asked as many as could to join in the procession. There would be no names on the new memorial, just the words *Lest we forget*. It wasn't just for the sons of local families, but for all the men of the camp. So many of them had worshipped in this church before they left on their journey to the front lines . . .

But now Kath was waiting impatiently for him to finish. She had worked out a plan of her own. As they'd arrived at the church, walking up from the gate, she had noticed a footpath crossing the churchyard and disappearing invitingly up some steps behind a stone wall. She wanted to see where it went. All week she had been doing her best not to be a nuisance, not to make Aunty Kitty cross, not to ask for things that would be difficult. It had been like being in a cage. And she had had hardly any chance to discover the secret corners of the village.

They would all take ages going out of the church and lining up for the procession outside the gate, she was sure. This was her last chance for a quick explore.

The choir filed out into the vestry. Aunty Kitty stood up, picking up her bag and gloves. Uncle Stan put away his glasses and snapped the case shut, gathering up the hymn books. Everyone began to move slowly towards the door, Kath too.

Out of the door then, into the light, and Uncle Stan way ahead, Aunty Kitty just in front of her, shaking the parson's hand and saying yes, thank you, she wasn't keeping too bad, though gettin' about any distance was a bother. Then Elsie Jarvis pushing through the crowd past Kath and putting a hand on Aunty Kitty's shoulder and saying something about a car and a lift, and Kath squashed in behind them both in the doorway, longing to move, run, jump, shout.

At last. Kath escaped. She dodged to one side and squeezed her way through to find the path.

Round the church it went, past tall gravestones splotched and greened with age, along under a spreading yew, and through a more overgrown patch with long grass and humps and bumps in the ground.

Here were the steps Kath had seen. Up them, racing behind the high stone wall, and then along a curving alley-way behind narrow cottage gardens, all cabbages, rotting heaps of leaves and battered chrysanthemums. On up the hill, and Kath was in a wood, the wood above the church, the ground thick with fallen leaves, from which jutted the solid grey elephant legs of beech trunks, fanning upward, spreading and interlacing into a roof of bare branches.

Panting, Kath flung herself down, and closed her eyes. She was hot, hotter than she had been for a long while. The sun was beating down on her face through the trees. She could feel its warmth, and hear a fly buzzing somewhere above her. The fly circled, now faint, now nearer. She need not go back yet. There was plenty of time.

SHE OPENED her eyes. The sun dazzled, shooting spears of light through the thick black-green lace of

leaves. She leant forward and loosened the laces on her boots, which felt tight and hot. They were getting too small, she needed new ones. Her pinafore was hot too, over her dress. She stood up, brushing herself free of twigs and bits of grass.

The air was filled with a heady scent – musty, sweet. Beside her was a large bush, its branches weighed down with white plates of blossom. Flies everywhere. And the young fresh green of slender beech trees beyond.

There was somewhere she ought to be, something she should be doing. What was it? She had lost it, could not think what it was. A stick lay on the grass by her feet. She picked it up, tapping it against the open palm of her left hand, frowning with the effort of remembering.

From down beyond the cottages, she could hear the faint thump of drums and the thin sound of distant brass. The band. That was it. That was

where she ought to be. She must hurry.

She ran down the path, past the back gardens behind the cottages, with their neat rows of green vegetables. A brown hen squawked away from her with a loud flurry of wings as she clattered by. She ran down, through the freshly mown churchyard, past the little yew, past the gravestones, down past the main side-door of the church and out under the lich-gate into the lane.

The band was louder now, she could hear it down the bottom of the dip.

She ran past the school and the school playground, rattling her stick across the railings as she went. No one in there today to tell her not to. Today was special.

Down the hill. Panting now. Music still playing. Not too late then. Past the tall oak tree next to the inn, and there they all were. Not yet gone. Crowds and crowds of soldiers, packed on to the platform of the station, with their kitbags and their rifles. She must have missed the march down there, they were all standing at ease now, some sitting on their bags, and the band was playing a tune she knew, Chalky was always whistling it, what was it? Oh yes, 'A Long Way to Tipperary'.

She scanned the faces under the caps for Tom, but there were so many, she could not find him. She could feel the tears coming, but she fought them back. 'No, Kitty,' he'd said, 'you mustn't cry, I'll be back, you'll see. But come and watch when we go, it'll be a grand sight, they'll have the regimental band playing an' all.'

And it was, it was a grand sight. She felt she could

burst with pride. There was a small crowd of folk from the village gathered outside the inn to watch. All people she knew by name. She wanted to shout out loud to them all, our Tom, our Tom's down there. Vince had already gone, was already in France; Vince so much older, almost one of the grown-ups. But Tom. Tom was full of silly jokes, could always make her laugh.

She felt a touch on her shoulder and twisted round to see who it was. It was the landlord of the inn, with a tray of pewter mugs in his hands. He held it down towards her, beer frothing over the rims.

'Kitty, my dear, d'you think you can take this down to the platform, let 'em share it round? 'Tis the least I can do.'

Immediately she is anxious about the money. 'How much must I ask for?'

'No, no, tell 'em 'tis my pleasure, an' I wish 'em all luck. But hurry now, or the train'll be 'ere. I'll fetch more.'

Take the tray then, cross the path, careful now, down the grass bank, somebody has seen her coming; there is pointing, laughter, a cheer. Kitty feels herself go scarlet, falters. But Tom is down there somewhere, even if she can't see him, he will be watching, will be proud of her. She steadies, keeps her eyes on the tray, feeling for the grass with her foot where it goes down. Safely on to the platform, the band louder now, beer slopping on to the tray, large hands reaching towards the tankards, tankards lifted, the tray lighter in her hands, the mugs

being passed along after a couple of gulps, as many as can be getting a share. Hot hands on her shoulders, and 'Thanks', 'Thanks', all around her.

The distant whistle of a train, and a sudden jostling and stamping, everyone standing up, lifting packs and rifles, where is the tray? Someone has taken it. Then an arm round her shoulders and almost lifted off her feet, held, hard, against rough serge and a hard webbing belt, a kiss pressed down on her forehead, a voice saying 'Goodbye, darlin'.' Released, back on her feet, somebody shouting orders, escape, retreat back up the bank, the tray forgotten, everyone waving now, train doors opening, soldiers getting in, doors slamming, heads and

shoulders coming out of carriage windows, arms waving, the station-master lowering his flag, the engine giving its first loud whoosh of steam.

Run now, just in time to get to the bridge to see the train go under it, past the oak tree, turn right up to the bridge, down the lane towards her a bicycle coming at breakneck speed, a delivery bike. It brakes, swerves wildly to miss her, skids on the gravelly lane and is down, on its side, and it's Chalky White on his butcher's round, hands and leg grazed, one trouser leg torn, scrambling to his feet and dashing to the wall with her to watch the carriage roofs go through below, then running to the other side to see the last of the carriages

disappear round the bend. Chalky furious, 'I missed it, I missed seein' 'em go!' Hands clenched, face white, cursing 'that durn cook up the big 'ouse, made me go back fer more scrag-end, said I 'adn't brought enough.'

And then the two of them, walking back down to pick up Chalky's bike and the paper packages which have fallen out of the front basket, and the band marching past them, back up the lane, while Chalky is muttering half to himself, half to Kitty, 'I got six months to wait, then I'm going, I'm going too, jus' as soon as I'm old enough.'

KATH CAN hear the band, somewhere up the top of the hill in the distance, the thump of the drums. She has taken too long exploring, the procession must have moved on ahead and be almost up to the war memorial. She had better hurry.

She runs up the lane, past the bus stop and the telephone box, past Uncle Stan and Aunty Kitty's cottage. Ah, there they all are, gathered at the top round the war memorial, a little crowd. There is Uncle Stan, with all his medals, and Frank, with his, and others with theirs; and a little further away, over the other side of the top road, Aunty Kitty, standing with Elsie Jarvis beside a car, while they watch. Someone is going to place a wreath of poppies, he stands holding it. Two people are carrying blue and gold banners. She recognizes one of the boys who were playing football, although he is now dressed in scout's uniform. He bears one of the banners.

'Where did you get to?' whispers Uncle Stan, reaching for her hand and pulling her to his side. 'I thought you was with Kitty, at the back, behind us all, followin'. And then I see 'er over there, come up in the car.'

Kath has no chance to answer. The band has stopped, and its members are sorting through music sheets for the next piece, and in the silence she hears the far mutter of an approaching tractor. It is coming from beyond the hedge, from the open field above the war memorial, the field which is crossed by the bridle-path where she and Uncle Stan walked.

The parson is saying something, but Kath is not listening. The noise gets louder, it is coming this way. The parson stops speaking and turns to look. Everybody is looking, even the bandsmen, even Aunty Kitty and Elsie Jarvis.

And then they see it. The big blue tractor from Bishop's Farm, coming along the bridle-path, and up in the cab is Kevin White, driving it. Nearer it comes, heading straight towards them, and then the front wheels turn and it is drawing up alongside the fence, and as it turns, Kath sees the trailer behind it. She reaches up and grabs Uncle Stan's arm, because in the trailer is a large armchair, wedged in with two old car tyres, and in the armchair is an old man, an old man with a shock of white hair. Kevin jumps down from the cab and scrambles into the trailer.

'You stay 'ere, alongside o' me,' says Chalky to him. 'I got a crackin' good view from up 'ere.' He raises an arm and waves to the crowd. 'You carry on.'

WHEN IT was over, Uncle Stan and Kath hurried across to the tractor and trailer.

'You made it, you old varmint,' said Stan, grinning broadly.

'Couldn't 'a done it without Kevin,' said Chalky, getting unsteadily to his feet. Kevin moved swiftly and Uncle Stan put out a hand to help him down out of the trailer. Elsie Jarvis joined them.

'You must've been fair shaken to pieces,' she said. 'Are you all right?'

'I am a bit shook up,' said Chalky, but he was smiling.

Elsie Jarvis said, 'You're not going back in that trailer, Chalky White. I'll drive you back in my car. We can all fit in somehow.'

But Aunty Kitty watched, her face set. Kath thought she heard her mutter 'Them Whites.'

Uncle Stan said sharply, 'Now hush up, Kitty, don' you go spoilin' things.' Kath was amazed to hear how angry he sounded. He turned to the others. 'Kevin 'ad better drive the tractor and trailer back to the farm, an' we'll go round the long way by the road. Kath can sit on my knee.'

BACK IN Chalky's cottage, with the big chair man-oeuvred in by Kevin and Uncle Stan, and restored to its place by the fire, Elsie Jarvis brews tea. Chalky sits down, and looks round at his visitors, smiling cheerfully. 'There,' he says, 'I done it. I come.'

'How did you get the chair on to the trailer?' asks Uncle Stan.

'Easy,' says Kevin. 'We all did it. Me and me mates.'

Chalky chuckles. 'And a right to-do it was. Nearly dropped it, they did.'

Kath cannot help noticing that although everybody else is talking happily, Aunty Kitty is silent. She accepts a cup of tea, and sits sipping it.

Uncle Stan says to Kath, 'You still 'aven't said. Where did you get to when we was all marchin' up the lane?'

Kath says, 'I was down by the station, by the oak tree, where the soldiers went from,' the words out before she knows what she is saying.

Uncle Stan says, 'What you want to be down by that scruffy old cutting for, down by the Oak Tree? You should 'a bin listenin' to the band, up with us.'

'But I heard the band,' says Kath, unsure, now that everyone is looking at her. 'It went past me.' She puts her hands up to her face, frowning, trying to sort out what has happened. 'There were all the soldiers . . .' She falters.

'Yes, yes,' cuts in Uncle Stan. 'All of us in the march. Old soldiers.'

'. . . and then . . . I was on the bridge, and the boy . . . the boy . . .' Who is the boy, the boy on the bicycle? She does not know, but he came down the hill towards her. 'He fell off,' she says. 'Fell off, when he swerved round me. And then he was angry, and said . . .' What had he said? She struggles to remember. Something about the big house? It doesn't seem right now.

And then Aunty Kitty speaks. She puts down her cup of tea and says, very quietly, from her corner, 'I remember a band, and a boy who fell off his bike. 'Twas a long time ago.'

She is looking intently at Chalky.

Chalky says, 'We was both on the bridge, you an' me. An' I was that mad, because I damn near missed seein' 'em all go, 'twas all because o' that durn cook up the big 'ouse. You must 'a bin jus' about Kath here's age . . .'

'Yes,' said Aunty Kitty. 'Oh my! And I mind how yer used ter tear about on that ramshackle delivery bike o' yours, always late, always showin' off 'ow fast you could go down the lane –'

'Oh ay,' says Chalky, 'but 'twern't showin' off. I 'ad that big a round, I *ad* ter go fast. All the way down to Tadbury an' back an' over to Bishop's Farm, miles an' miles –' He waves an arm wide, forgetting his mug of tea, which slops over on to the carpet by the fire. Aunty Kitty is up to fetch a cloth and across the room at once, crouched at Chalky's feet and mopping with one hand, barely noticing what she is doing, her face lifted towards Chalky. 'You wasn't livin' at Bishop's Farm then, you was up Pearce's. An' we was in the cottage along the way, the one that's bin pulled down, where them two bungalows is now . . .' and she is off, reminding him how it was then for them both, there is no holding her now, she cannot stop talking.

Kath sits, trying to piece together her own thoughts. She has tried to tell them what she has seen, but they have not understood. Perhaps it is better that they should not? Perhaps she is in some way meant to keep it to herself?

She thinks about the station and the departing train. The station must have been where the Green now is, and the overgrown bank is the old cutting through which the railway ran. There must have been a bridge where the line went under the lane.

Aunty Kitty is saying to Chalky, as if in echo of her thought, 'But do you remember, we did see it go? You was jus' in time to see the train go round the corner, an' then you was in such a pickle, yer leg bleedin' an' yer trousers all tore, an' all them parcels o' meat all over the road . . .' She is shaking her head, sitting back on her heels with the wet cloth in one hand, half laughing, and, it suddenly comes to Kath, half crying. 'Oh Chalky,' she is saying through her tears, 'you always was in such a tearin' hurry –'

Chalky says, 'You weren't goin' so slow yerself, dashin' out across the lane like that without any warning. 'Twas lucky I see'd yer when I did.'

But Aunty Kitty will not be halted. '. . . Late fer seein'·'em off, late on yer rounds, an' now late this mornin' an' interruptin' everything –'

Kevin breaks in. 'That weren't 'is fault. You all got to the cross much sooner than you'd said.'

Aunty Kitty stands up. 'An' you're jus' the same, Kevin, the same as he was, always racin' around, goin' down the lane on yer board.'

Chalky says, 'Kitty Poulshott – savin' yer presence, Stan, 'cos that's 'ow I always thinks of 'er – Kitty Poulshott, I come because of you, an' Tom, an' Vince. 'Tweren't that easy, as Kevin an' the others 'll tell you. Now jus' you hush up. Kevin's a good lad, an' 'e's right. Jus' you remember that. Come to that now, there's some as is late an' in a tearin' hurry, but they gets there in the end, an' there's some as never sets out. Where were you, I'd like ter know, when

73

your little Kath 'ere was all of a fuss in the call-box, tryin' ter ring 'ome?'

Aunty Kitty stands silent, staring at him. It is a long silence.

Kevin says, 'I 'ad ter do it for 'er. She didn' know what to do.'

Kath says quickly, 'Yes, he did, he helped me.'

'Well,' says Aunty Kitty, 'well.' And she sits down in a chair, looking first at one and then at the other, shaking her head in wonder.

'I didn't want to tell you,' says Kath bravely.

'Oh my,' says Aunty Kitty, and her eyes fill with tears again.

She drops the cloth and wipes her eyes with the back of one hand, blindly holding out the other

towards Uncle Stan for a handkerchief. Uncle Stan
fumbles to find one, but Chalky lurches to his feet
and is by her side, one arm round her shoulders.

'Oh, you Whites,' says Aunty Kitty, 'you Whites,'
sniffing back the tears just like a little girl. She
shakes her head. And then she says, so muffled in a
sob that Kath is not sure she hears right, 'Chalky.
About Tom an' that. I'm sorry. 'An' I'm glad you're
still here.'

Kath does not hear what Chalky says, because
Uncle Stan has found a handkerchief and moves a
chair scraping across the floor in order to give it to
Aunty Kitty. But it must be all right, because after
she has blown her nose, Aunty Kitty has cheered up
and is smiling, first at Chalky, then at Uncle Stan,

and her face is all crumpled and pink again like one of her little apples.

MUCH, MUCH later that afternoon, when they had said goodbye to Chalky and gone home and had lunch, Kath's parents arrived in the car to fetch her back to London.

Kath flew into her father's arms. 'Hey, steady on,' he said.

'Where's Mum?' asked Kath.

'She's just getting out of the car,' said her father. 'Why the rush?'

At that moment Kath's mother came in through the door, holding a pot plant swathed in Cellophane paper. She gave it to Aunty Kitty, and then kissed Kath.

Aunty Kitty made tea, but after Kath's father had drunk one cup he said they mustn't stop, he wanted to get everyone home before dark.

Kath hugged Uncle Stan and Aunty Kitty goodbye, and promised to come back soon, and gave Patch a special farewell stroke.

As they drove up the lane, Kath's mother turned her head and asked her 'Was it all right? Did you have a nice time? Any good deeds?'

'Yes,' said Kath, but she did not want to say more. Somehow she knew that everything that had happened was between her and Aunty Kitty and Chalky White, and should stay that way. And maybe Uncle Stan and Kevin as well. She would come back and see them again, she was sure.

The car slowed at the T-junction at the top of the

lane, and turned left past the stone cross. Kath could just see the wreath propped at its foot, and as they drove along the top road towards the motorway and home, she found herself humming a tune, the hymn they had sung in church.

> Time, like an ever-rolling stream,
> Bears all its sons away.
> They fly forgotten, as a dream
> Dies at the break of day.

One by one she went over the extraordinary things that had happened to her that morning, and felt again in memory the rough serge, the hard webbing belt, herself held and the kiss pressed down on her forehead. Forgotten as a dream . . .

Not by me, thought Kath, not as long as I live, not ever.